OAKIE DOKIE'S
HAPPY ROOTS

"Connecting children to nature connects them to God...naturally"

Young Bark Buddie Oak Tree discovers the six roots of growing up happy

CONSTANCE NELSON

WestBow Press books may be ordered through booksellers or by contacting:

WestBow Press
A Division of Thomas Nelson & Zondervan
1663 Liberty Drive
Bloomington, IN 47403
www.westbowpress.com
844-714-3454

Because of the dynamic nature of the Internet, any web addresses or links contained in this book may have changed since publication and may no longer be valid. The views expressed in this work are solely those of the author and do not necessarily reflect the views of the publisher, and the publisher hereby disclaims any responsibility for them.

Scripture taken from the International Children's Bible®. Copyright © 1986, 1988, 1999 by Thomas Nelson. Used by permission. All rights reserved.

ISBN: 978-1-9736-8431-2 (sc)
ISBN: 978-1-6642-1784-3 (hc)
ISBN: 978-1-9736-8432-9 (e)

Library of Congress Control Number: 2020901172

Print information available on the last page.

WestBow Press rev. date: 01/11/2021

WestBow
PRESS®
A DIVISION OF THOMAS NELSON
& ZONDERVAN

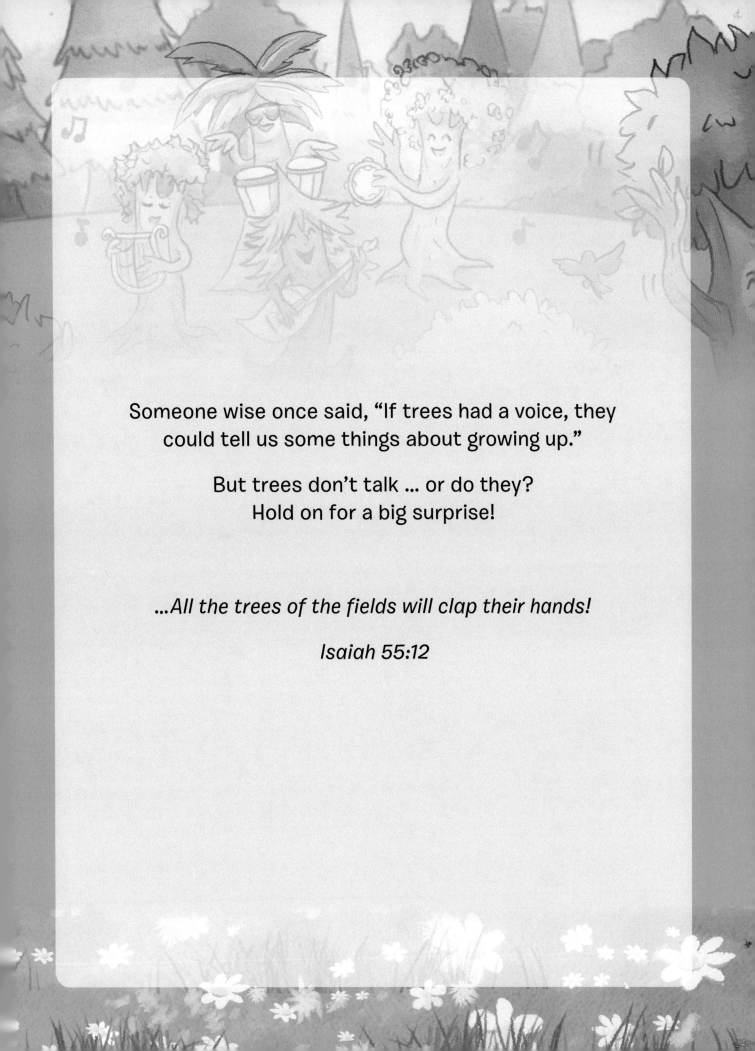

Someone wise once said, "If trees had a voice, they could tell us some things about growing up."

But trees don't talk ... or do they?
Hold on for a big surprise!

...All the trees of the fields will clap their hands!

Isaiah 55:12

See that spunky little Oak tree over there by the daisy field, playing with squirrels and a bright red bird perched on his branch? That's Oakie Dokie, one of the young Bark Buddie Tree® sprouts.

Oakie Dokie is a young sprout in the Bark Buddie Tree® family. They're not your ordinary bashful, backyard trees. They're trunk yappin' talking that is, root tappin' dancing that is, leaf clappin' trees on a mission to root-for-kids like you! They live in a special hidden place, the Secret Valley.

One day in early spring, Big Bark Buddie, the friendly guardian tree in the Secret Valley, was looking on as some of the young sprouts were playing a fun game of limbo. He noticed Oakie Dokie was not taking turns.

Do you always take turns?

Big Bark root scooted over, gently putting his limb around Oakie, "Let's take a walk in the woods young sprout, let's have a tree to tree talk about roots."

Do you like to take walks in the woods?

The young sprouts in the Secret Valley know to listen when wise Big Bark Buddie Tree speaks. Looking down at his roots, "What do you mean Big Bark? Is there something wrong with my roots?"

Stopping by a sparkling stream to stick their roots in the cool water, Big Bark playfully splashes Oakie, getting his attention, "When you put down strong roots, you will not be so easily talked into doing wrong things. **Happy Roots** keep you on the right path in life."

...He is strong, like a tree planted by a river.

Psalm 1:3

"All young sprouts, even the people kind, need six strong roots to grow up happy. The **first Happy Root** is **TRUSTWORTHINESS** – that means being honest and courageous to do what's right even when it's hard." Oakie started to perk up and listen.

Can you think of a time when you did the right thing?

Big Bark stretched out in the sun, dangling his roots in the stream and Oakie followed, "The **second Happy Root** is **RESPECT**, that means listening to what others have to say and thanking them!"

Suddenly, a big fat crawdad jumped and pinched one of Oakie's roots..."OUCH, crawdaddy!" Little Oakie looked a little sheepish, "Uh oh, I think my **RESPECT** root needs to be pinched."

Big Bark reassured Oakie, "We all make mistakes, but the more you practice **RESPECT**, the easier it will get and the less pinching we need."

Can you name someone you should say "thank you" to more often?

Oakie hopped up and started kicking up his roots in a happy root scootin' jig. "What's the **third Happy Root** Big Bark? I'm diggin' this trunk talk!"

Big Bark chuckled at Oakie's funny jig, "The **third Happy Root** is **RESPONSIBILITY**, a big word that means being dependable, doing what you say you will do." Oakie stuck out his trunk proudly, "Hey, I'm dependable, I'm an Oak tree!" Big Bark nods his approval with a big green thumbs up.

Can you make a big thumbs up?

As they root scooted along the edge of the woods, they stopped by a butterfly picnic in progress. A pretty bright yellow butterfly landed on Oakie, tickling his trunk. He giggled. Big Bark gave Oakie a big grin, "That's the **fourth Happy Root** right there, showing you **CARE** by welcoming a visitor.

Can you name some ways you show care for people and animals?

Oakie's eyes got bright and big, "I did, didn't I? Hey, my roots are growing!"

"Superb sprout! ...now, Oakie, the **fifth Happy Root** is **FAIRNESS** - that means not to be a sore loser and to think about how your actions will affect others!"

Oakie looked down at his roots, mumbling, "Uh oh, I might've pouted once or twice when I didn't get my way."

Big Bark reassuringly patted Oakie as if to say, "it's ok".

Have you ever pouted when you didn't get your way?

"OK Oakie, the **sixth Happy Root** is **CITIZENSHIP** – meaning we should do our share to take care of our school, church, family, neighborhood and friends!"

Oakie's eyes opened wide, "Sometimes, I sweep leaves to help prevent forest fires in the Secret Valley!" Big Bark gave two big green thumbs up this time, "That's *TREE*-mendous, Oakie!"

Can you name some things you can do to help out around your home, school, church and community?

Big Bark, pulled out a book from his trunk pocket, "All of these **SIX HAPPY ROOTS** will help you grow up strong and HAPPY! The MAIN thing is, be sure you are growing all of your **happy roots** deep down into the good dirt of THIS **Good Book** and pray every day!"

Oakie carefully took the book and pauses, "Can I say a prayer right now Big Bark?"

Big Bark nodded yes and they bowed down. As little Oakie humbly prayed, a tear rolled down his trunk to the ground, watering a seed that suddenly sprouts!

"I'm sorry God for the wrong things I've done. From now on, will you please help me to grow strong happy roots and share Your Words with all of the Bark Buddie Trees® and kids too? With your help, I know we can all grow up together to make the world a happier place. Amen!"

You can say this prayer too!

Big Bark waved his limbs for all the Secret Valley to come and celebrate this "*TREE*-mendous" awakening for Oakie, "It's time for us to do our happy dance and have some root scootin', leaf clappin' fun with the Bark Buddie Band's favorite songs."

Oakie Dokie, the Bark Buddie Band, along with Nutquacker squirrel, his best friend, broke out into their root scootin' boogie "root-ine" as they sang the song, "Happy Roots Grow Happy Fruits!"

GROW UP HAPPY!

...the Spirit gives love, joy, peace, patience, kindness, goodness, faithfulness, gentleness and self-control.

Galatians 5:22

Printed in the United States
By Bookmasters